To: Mary

Always be friendly
and Kind!

Diane Davies
2021

Book 2

Life in the Neck
Squirrel Trouble

Written by
Diane Davies

Illustrated by
Margarita Sikorskaia

BEAVER'S
POND
PRESS

For all kids anywhere, at any age,
who love making forts out of anything!
Especially Eli!
—DD

To my son, Ilya,
who taught me how to live in harmony
with all creatures.
—MS

Edited by Alicia Ester
Illustrated by Margarita Sikorskaia

ISBN: 978-1-64343-964-8
Library of Congress Catalog Number: 2019906456
Printed in the United States of America
First Printing: 2020
24 23 22 21 20   5 4 3 2 1

Cover and interior design by Sara J Weingartner

Beaver's Pond Press, Inc.
7108 Ohms Lane
Edina, MN 55439-2129

BEAVER'S
POND
PRESS

(952) 829-8818
www.BeaversPondPress.com

To order, visit www.ItascaBooks.com or call (952) 345-4488.
Reseller discounts available.

For classroom ideas and teaching suggestions,
visit **www.DianeDavies.com**.

Chapter 1

The cold rains arrived shortly after the ravaging fire that damaged the long narrow strip of land called the Neck.

Blackened trees with fallen branches crisscrossed the forest floor. In the cornfield, a dark path of burned stalks ran from the pine trees to the river, showing how the fire had traveled in the wind.

One small flame had left behind so much destruction.

Delaney, the whitetail deer, and Rocket, the cottontail rabbit, had made it to safety with their families thanks to Cardinal Red's brave warning flight. Even Old Coyote had survived. After saving Delaney, he disappeared into the forest once again.

A few weeks later, Eli, the young boy living at the end of the drive, was putting the finishing touches on his fort with his dad. They had worked all summer cutting down trees, debarking the logs, and shimming (filling up and moving) things in place as the log cabin rose in the forest.

The plank floor, real glass windows, front porch, and metal roofing were all in place. The welcome sign was even nailed to the door.

Because of the wind's direction, Eli's fort escaped any danger from the fire.

The curious animals of the Neck had watched as the fort was built over the summer. Delaney and Rocket stayed well hidden in the trees. As the boy and his dad left each day, the two friends scampered across the meadow to peer into the shelter of the fort.

"Hey, Rocket, what are those perky, chattering little guys inside?" asked Delaney.

"They look like red squirrels to me," replied Rocket. "See the rusty red fur on their backs and the white on their bellies? They have extremely fluffy tails and are the smallest squirrels in the forest. They only weigh ounces, but have a lot of energy and like to be busy and bossy."

"Where do they live?"

"It looks like they've made a leaf nest in the crotch of the maple tree behind the fort. Do you see it?" asked Rocket.

"Oooooooooh! They are so adorable," crooned Delaney. "Yes, I see the nest."

Chapter 2

Mr. and Mrs. Red Squirrel, along with their three children, Chatter, Whistle, and Squeak, had already found the comforts of Eli's fort to their liking. They were busy storing up a cache (secure supply) of food for the winter: pinecones, acorns, mushrooms, and maple seeds. Every little nook, crack, and cranny inside the fort was stuffed full.

Eli saw the cache growing as well. He'd sweep out as many nuts and seeds as he could and still find growing piles each day.

"What's making that mess?" he asked his dad.

"I think it's red squirrels," Dad replied. "They're getting ready for the cold winter by storing food in your fort. Red squirrels often bury seeds and nuts underground too," he explained. "They can be real pests. When they start eating that food is when the mess will get really bad. They'll leave piles, up to a foot high, of shredded pinecones and husks and hulls of the seeds and nuts."

"What do I do now, Dad?" asked Eli.

"Well, I guess you keep cleaning up the squirrels' mess until you find a way to get them out of your fort," answered Dad.

The two hurried off to their computer to look for the answer online. Meanwhile, Delaney and Rocket were off to warn the squirrel family of what might be ahead.

STEP-BY-STEP GUIDE FOR GETTING RID OF SQUIRRELS

Step 1: Inspect the entire building and find all entry holes.

Step 2: As you find them, seal them shut with steel mesh, which squirrels cannot chew through.

Step 3: Mount a repeater trap or a one-way door on the main hole.

Step 4: If you use a trap, remove and relocate caught squirrels. If you use a one-way door, just wait two or three days.

SUCCESS: When you don't hear the scurrying noises and the piles of food don't reappear, you've done it.

FAILURE: If you still have squirrels, it means you failed Steps 1 and 2. You must find the remaining holes.

Step 5: Optional. Clean and disinfect the building.

DO NOT! Use rat poison.

DO NOT! Use any kind of repellent spray, powder, sound box, or flashing lights. These gimmicks fail.

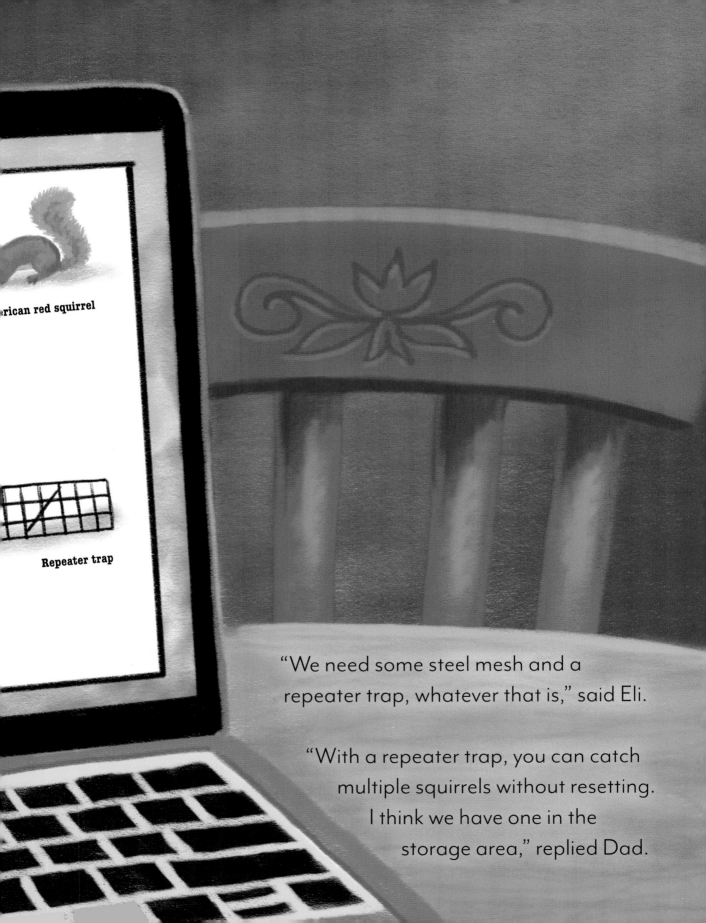

rican red squirrel

Repeater trap

"We need some steel mesh and a
repeater trap, whatever that is," said Eli.

"With a repeater trap, you can catch
multiple squirrels without resetting.
I think we have one in the
storage area," replied Dad.

Chapter 3

Armed with his supplies, Eli
headed out to the fort to start
the squirrel removal process
he had read about.

Step 1: Check for holes. The
spaces between logs, where
sunlight filtered into the fort,
were humongous! Every wall
looked the same. The ceiling
was sealed tight because of
the metal roof.

Step 2: Seal the holes. Eli figured there was not enough steel mesh in the world to fill all the cracks and holes he saw. His supply was quickly gone and he was still on the first hole!

He used whatever he could find
in and around the fort—bark strips,
Styrofoam pieces, dried leaves, and
cornstalks. Satisfied that he had most
of the holes filled, he went on to Step
3. Using peanuts and peanut butter as
bait, he went on to set up his trap by the
door, the biggest hole of all. He decided
to leave the door open just a crack so
the squirrels would take the bait.

"Okay, guys. I've got you now!"
muttered Eli as he left for the day.

Thanks to Delaney and Rocket, Chatter, Whistle, and Squeak secretly observed Eli's every move, laughing nervously at his hard work but admiring him for it too.

They watched him walk down the hill toward home and then set to work themselves.

They quickly pushed out the leaves and cornstalks from the cracks and carried in more pinecones, nuts, and mushrooms, piling them high. The three squirrel siblings, satisfied with their own work, entered the trap and enjoyed the treats that Eli had left for them. Realizing they could not get out, they snuggled down together and went to sleep.

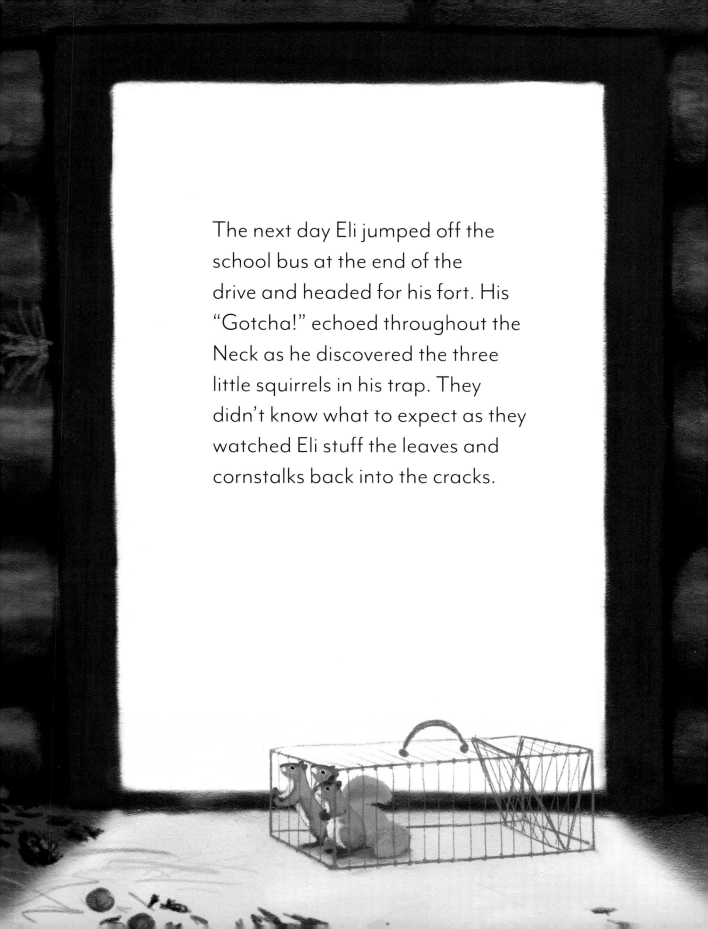

The next day Eli jumped off the school bus at the end of the drive and headed for his fort. His "Gotcha!" echoed throughout the Neck as he discovered the three little squirrels in his trap. They didn't know what to expect as they watched Eli stuff the leaves and cornstalks back into the cracks.

On to Step 4. He carefully picked up the trap and walked across the meadow, over the cornfield, and into the woods above the river. He opened the trap and let Chatter, Whistle, and Squeak scamper away, thinking he had seen the last of them as he let them out. Arriving back at the fort, Eli reset the trap, just in case more squirrels were around, and headed home.

Chapter 4

Mr. and Mrs. Red Squirrel watched from their nest in the maple tree as Chatter, Whistle, and Squeak quickly ran back into the fort and began the whole series of actions over again. The three ended up in the trap once more. This little game of Eli finding them, letting them go, and the young squirrels running back went on for a whole week.

When Eli jumped off the bus on Friday afternoon, he decided he'd had enough of the game. He would write his own Step 6 for the STEP-BY-STEP GUIDE FOR GETTING RID OF SQUIRRELS.

STEP 6

If all other steps
fail —

Learn to live with
the Squirrels

Eli and his new pals, Chatter, Whistle, and Squeak, did just that— they learned to share the fort for the time being. The trap was put back into storage, the leaves and cornstalks were left on the floor, out of the cracks, and the peanuts and peanut butter treat were delivered daily by Eli when he came home.

Mr. and Mrs. Red Squirrel and their children grew very fat as the winter progressed—especially Mrs. Red Squirrel!

When spring came, it would be time to start the list all over again.